AF674433

The Adventures of Pirates

The Skull and Bone Pirates

Om KIDZ

An imprint of Om Books International

Once upon a time, there were a group of pirates who had saved a sea monster from certain death. Pleased with the pirates, the sea monster had granted them the boon of invisibility.

As a result, the pirate ship became totally invisible and only the skull and bones of these pirates were visible. As the pirates sailed the seas and robbed ships off their valuables, they terrorised everyone. No one could see their ship and the sailors thought that pirate ghosts were attacking them.

These pirates were known as the Skull and Bone Pirates. But, there was one catch to this boon of invisibility. Only if you were a pirate yourself, you could spot the invisible pirate ship as well as the skull and bone pirates.

The king of the land was worried as the fishermen and the merchant ships kept complaining about these strange pirates who kept attacking them.

"How can I catch these pirates?" he said to his chief minister worriedly. "They seem to be invisible just as their ship!"

"I have questioned two people who have seen this ship, Your Majesty!" the chief minister replied.

"Who are they?" the king asked in surprise.

"They are two other pirates who are in our prison," the chief minister replied. "It appears that only pirates can see this ship and its skull and bone crew."

"There is some hope then," the king cried. "What do you suggest, O wise one?"

"There is only one option, Your Highness!" the chief minister replied. "Set a thief to catch a thief!"

“Please do not speak in riddles and explain your plan!” the king said impatiently.

“We must send a group of pirates to capture the skull and bone pirates. That is the only way,” the chief minister offered.

"But how?" the king exclaimed.

"We have some pirates in captivity who have agreed to do so," the chief minister replied.

"But can we trust them?" the king asked.

“We have to grant them a royal pardon if they succeed and include them in our armed forces,” the chief minister replied.

“But will they succeed?” the king asked doubtfully.

“I have a back-up plan,” the chief minister replied.

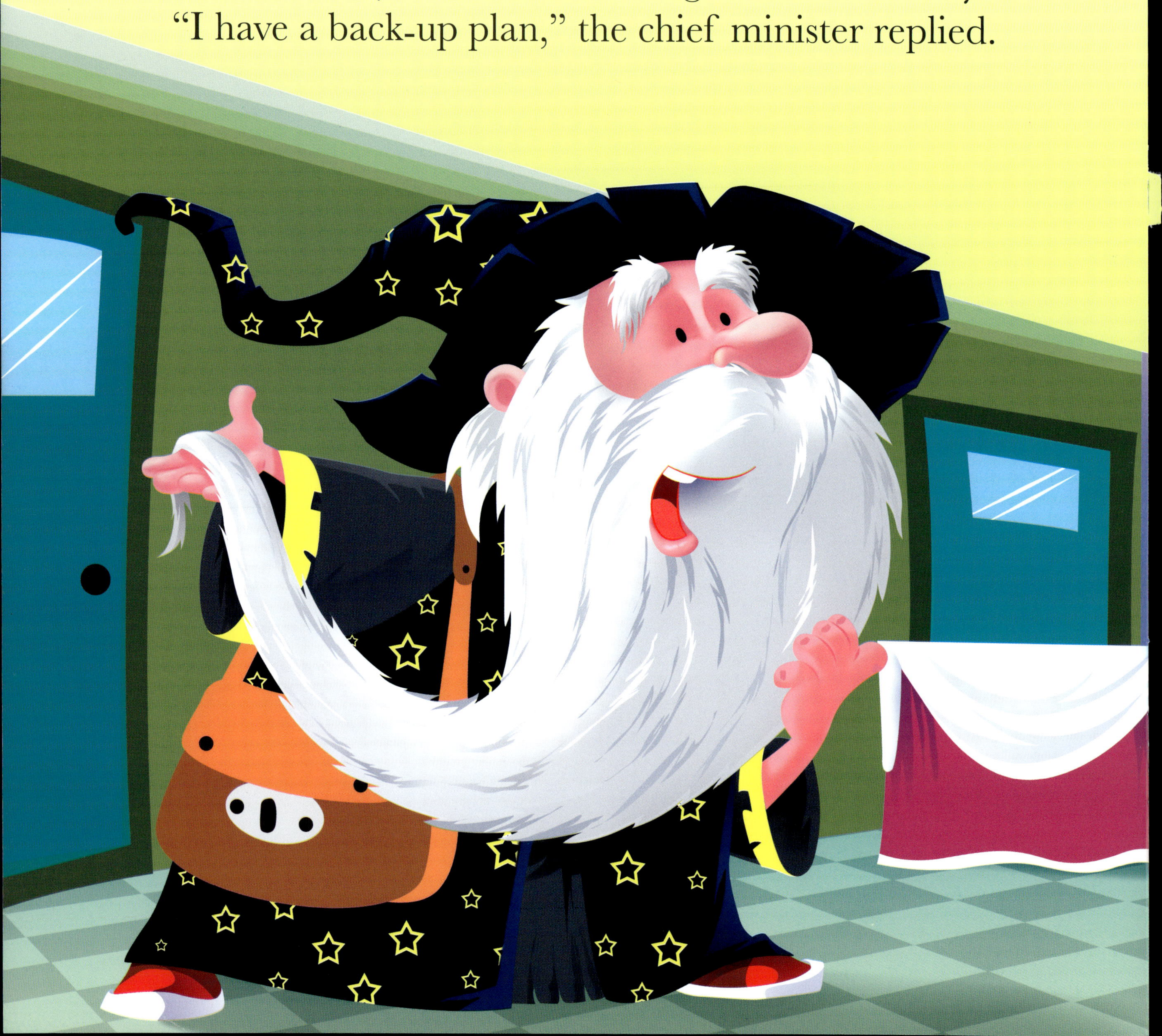

"I trust you completely," the king said and left to attend other urgent matters of state. The chief minister immediately called upon the old wizard Mysterio.

"I require something that makes invisible things visible!" the chief minister ordered Mysterio.

"There is a powder that will take me a week to create," Mysterio replied.

"You have three days!" the chief minister replied.

After a week, ten pirates were released from the king's prison and sailed to the sea in one of the king's finest warships.

They were armed to the teeth and followed by another warship boarded by the chief minister and other warriors. The king's pirates spotted the ship of the Skull and Bone Pirates easily even though the chief minister and his men could not see it.

The king's pirates attacked the ship and the chief minister could see them fighting the enemy. But all he could see were skull and bones fighting his pirates and since he could not see the ship, it seemed that the men were battling each other while suspended in the air.

"Quickly!" the chief minister ordered his men who rowed in their boats and sprinkled Mysterio's magic powder all over the pirate ship; it soon became visible. The soldiers then boarded the pirate ship and sprinkled magic powder all over so that the pirates were visible.

"Take no prisoners!" the chief minister ordered. "Kill them all before they disappear!"

The Skull and Bone Pirates were killed. True to his word, the pirates who had fought for the king received a royal pardon and served the king till the day they died.